Mary Marony
and the
Chocolate Surprise

Suzy Kline

Mary Marony
and the
Chocolate Surprise

Illustrations by Blanche Sims

G. P. PUTNAM'S SONS
NEW YORK

Special appreciation for
my editor, Anne O'Connell,
Roald Dahl's *Charlie and the Chocolate Factory*, and
my second-graders who inspired this story.

Text copyright © 1995 by Suzy Kline
Illustrations copyright © 1995 by Blanche Sims
All rights reserved. This book, or parts thereof,
may not be reproduced in any form without
permission in writing from the publisher.
G. P. Putnam's Sons, a division of
The Putnam & Grosset Group,
200 Madison Avenue, New York, NY 10016.
G. P. Putnam's Sons, Reg. U.S. Pat. & Tm. Off.
Published simultaneously in Canada.
Printed in the United States of America
Designed by Donna Mark and Marikka Tamura.
Text set in Sabon.
Library of Congress Cataloging-in-Publication Data
Kline, Suzy. Mary Marony and the chocolate surprise /
Suzy Kline : illustrations by Blanche Sims.   p.   cm.
Summary: Mary decides it's all right to cheat
to make sure she wins a special lunch with her
favorite teacher, but the results of her dishonesty
end up surprising the whole second-grade class.
[1. Honesty—Fiction. 2. Schools—Fiction.
3. Teacher-student relationships—Fiction.
4. Stuttering—Fiction.] I. Sims, Blanche, ill. II. Title.
PZ7.K6797Man 1995 [Fic]—dc20 94-23600 CIP AC

ISBN 0-399-22829-2

7 9 10 8

Dedicated with all my love
to Rufus

Happy Twenty-fifth Anniversary

Contents

1

Mean Marvin!

Mrs. Bird closed her book, *Charlie and the Chocolate Factory,* and took off her reading glasses. "Now it's time to celebrate this wonderful story with some fizzy-lifting lemonade!"

Mary Marony leaned forward as she watched her teacher open a large can of frozen pink lemonade. She liked the way the icy glob slowly dropped into the glass pitcher.

Plop!

When her teacher added some seltzer, the pink drink foamed up and fizzed. *What fun!* Mary thought.

"Don't forget to burp, everybody," Marvin Higgins blurted out. "When you drink Fizzy Lifting, you fill up with gas bubbles. You float up in the air and hit the ceiling. The only way you can come back down again is to burp."

Mrs. Bird stopped pouring the pink lemonade.

"That's what Willie Wonka said in the book," Marvin pointed out.

"YEAH!" a lot of the students said.

Mary could tell their teacher was worried. The paper cup was shaking in her hand. No teacher wanted a burping festival.

Mary turned and glared at Marvin. "Can't you see you're muh-muh-making Muh-mrs. Bird unhappy?"

"No, Muh-muh-mary Muh-muh-marony!" Marvin snickered.

Mary gritted her teeth. Marvin just wouldn't stop. He loved teasing her about stuttering on *M* words. When he wasn't bugging *her,* he was bugging the teacher.

"You're right, Marvin," Mrs. Bird said. "I'm glad you remember the story details. However . . . we'll . . . eh . . . leave the burping part out."

Marvin and Fred Heinz booed.

Mary folded her arms. Those two dumb boys were spoiling another fun activity. It wasn't fair!

Mrs. Bird asked Audrey Tang and Elizabeth Conway, the day's helpers, to pass out the Fizzy Lifting.

When everyone had their own paper cup, Mrs. Bird made a toast. "To Charlie Bucket!"

And then after a moment of drinking, Marvin burped. *"Buuuuuuuuuuuurp!"* It was long and low and rumbled.

Mrs. Bird shot Marvin a look but she didn't say anything.

Fred was next. *"BUUUUUUURP!"* His was so loud the class started laughing. After Pablo and Robert each took a turn, Mrs. Bird got angry and waved one hand in the air. "All right, class, that will be enough!"

Just as she brought her hand down, she knocked Amol's cup of lemonade onto the floor.

"Oh, I'm sorry, Amol!" Mrs. Bird said.

Mary grabbed her blue napkin, knelt down, and started helping the teacher wipe the sticky mess off the floor.

"Thank you, Mary," Mrs. Bird said.

Mary smiled. Then she noticed Marvin and Fred were staring at Mrs. Bird's hair.

"Look at those gray roots!" Marvin whispered. "Mrs. Bird's not a redhead. She's a grayhead."

Mary covered her mouth. She never thought her teacher was old.

Until now.

When the teacher got up and walked away, Marvin started singing:

On top of ol' Smokey
I saw Mrs. Bird's head.
There's thousands of gray hairs.
She dyes her hair red.

Mary gritted her teeth. Marvin could be so mean. She remembered something her mom said once: "Mary! Your messy room is making me turn gray!"

Marvin was the reason Mrs. Bird was turning gray.

Mary felt bad for her teacher. She took a piece of paper out of her binder and started writing.

Dear Mrs. Bird,

I'm sorry some of the kids
started berping when you gave
us Fizzee Liffing. Your my
favrit techer. We always do fun
things.

Love,
Mary

P.S. Your pritty.

Just as Mary dropped the letter on the
teacher's desk, Mrs. Bird called out,
"MARVIN HIGGINS!"

Mary turned around. Marvin was
holding the classroom guinea pig on his
lap at the audio table.

He had the earphones on the guinea
pig's head.

"Fluffy likes Beethoven," Marvin
said.

Mrs. Bird took the pet and returned him to his wire cage. "If we don't treat our animals nicely, we won't be able to have any."

As soon as the teacher turned her back, Marvin stuck his tongue out at her.

Ohhhhhh, Mary thought. There was only one word to describe Marvin. It was a word in her dad's crossword puzzle.

Nincompoop!

2

The Golden Tickets

The next morning when Mary came to class, she noticed Mrs. Bird had written something on the chalkboard in big yellow block letters:

5 GOLDEN TICKETS

Mary also noticed something on the little round table in front of the room. A cloth was draped over a cookie tray.

Mary could tell there was something underneath.

What was it?

Mrs. Bird explained. "Because we loved *Charlie and the Chocolate Factory* so much, I've decided we should have one more special activity to celebrate the book. Just before lunch, I will ask everyone to choose one chocolate bar from this tray."

The class watched as Mrs. Bird took the cloth off the cookie tray.

"Oooooooh," Pablo oohed.

Mary stared at the mountain of chocolate bars wrapped in silver foil and shiny brown paper.

"Inside five of these," the teacher said, "is a golden ticket. If the candy you select has a golden ticket, you will have lunch with me in the classroom."

The class cheered and clapped.

Lunch with my favorite teacher, Mary thought. *Yes!*

"We'll have double-cheese pizza and make our own sundaes," Mrs. Bird said. "I'll send notes home with the five winners explaining to your parents why you won't need to bring or buy lunch that day."

Mary raised her hand. "What about Elizabeth? She's absent."

Mrs. Bird nodded. "She'll get the candy bar that's left. Will you take it to her after school, Mary, since you live nearby?"

Mary couldn't wait!

Audrey leaned across the aisle and started a conversation with Mary. "I'm never lucky at things like this."

"I am!" Marvin butted in. "I'm on a winning streak. Just last week, I put my name in the public library raffle and won a paperback."

"Was the book good?" Mary asked.

"Haven't read it."

Mary made a face. Marvin didn't deserve to have lunch with Mrs. Bird. He'd just spoil it.

Marvin continued bragging. "Two weeks ago, I won a poetry contest for seven- to nine-year-olds in the newspaper."

"You told us that before," Audrey reminded him.

"What did you get?" Fred asked.

"A certificate with a gold sticker. Everybody loves gold. Right, Muh-muh-mary?"

Audrey shook her finger at Marvin. "You shouldn't tease people who stutter. It's mean."

Marvin smiled. "I think it's fun."

Mary turned around. She didn't feel like talking. She couldn't wait to get her candy bar. It would be so WONDERFUL to get a golden ticket inside.

Fred blurted out, "Can we open our chocolate bar right away?"

"No," Mrs. Bird said. "Not until we get back from lunch. I want you to experience the same feelings Charlie Bucket had when he was waiting and hoping for his golden ticket. When you understand what Charlie went through, you'll have *empathy* for him."

Mary watched the teacher write the new word, *empathy,* on chart paper.

"One hour of waiting!" Marvin complained. "That's not fair."

"It's sweet waiting, Marvin." Mrs. Bird smiled. "Everyone will at least get some chocolate."

At eleven-thirty that morning, Mrs. Bird picked up the tray of chocolate bars. "Now, before you come up and choose your candy bar, I want us all to agree on one thing."

Mrs. Bird stopped talking.

She wanted everyone's attention.

When the room was quiet, she continued. "We'll congratulate the winners and not have any hard feelings."

"You mean 'no sour grapes,'" Fred replied. "That's what my dad always says."

Mrs. Bird nodded.

One by one the students came up, checked the pile of candy, and returned

to their seats with one chocolate bar each.

By eleven forty-five, every desk except Elizabeth's had a candy bar on it. Mrs. Bird kept hers.

Marvin picked up his chocolate and sniffed it. "Mmmmmmm, I can smell the pizza."

Mary glared at Marvin. He couldn't be lucky three times in a row! First the library, then the poetry contest, and now?

The thought made Mary's stomach turn.

Mary ran her finger over the silver foil and shiny brown paper. She looked at the neatly folded corners.

Did *her bar* have a golden ticket?

Mary's curiosity was killing her.

So was Marvin's. Mary could see he was sliding part of the paper label off.

"Don't touch the candy yet," Mrs. Bird warned. "I wouldn't want anyone peeking ahead of time."

Marvin made a face.

"Let's list on the board all the words we can make from the word *chocolate*," Mrs. Bird suggested. "Who can think of one?"

Nobody raised a hand. Everyone was fiddling with their bar of chocolate. Some people were smelling theirs.

Finally Audrey raised her hand. "*Late.*"

"Good!" Mrs. Bird wrote it with brown chalk on the board.

"*Cat,*" Fred blurted out.

"*Loco,*" Pablo said. "I don't like waiting to open my chocolate bar. It's driving me *loco en la cabeza.*" Then he whirled his finger and pointed to his head.

The class laughed.

By the time the lunch bell rang, there were thirteen words on the board. One had six letters.

"Good job! Let's line up now," Mrs. Bird said.

Everyone got their jacket except Marvin and Mary.

Mary was standing at the end of the line, dreaming. She could picture herself eating pizza and talking about Willie Wonka's chocolate factory.

Marvin was looking for his milk money in his desk.

When he finally joined the line in the hall, everyone was chanting, "Gold-en tick-et, gold-en tick-et, gold-en tick-et."

Marvin didn't chant with the rest of the class. He had his own verse:

> *On top of ol' Smokey*
> *It ain't very cold.*
> *I found me some pizza*
> *All wrapped up in gold.*

Marvin's song reminded Mary of the smoke alarm that went off when her mom was cooking.

All she could do was plug her ears.

3

The Golden Switch

Mary and Audrey got their trays of hot food and sat down at their lunchroom table. They were so excited about the golden tickets they couldn't talk about anything else. Not even the chicken nuggets, which were also golden that day.

"I figured it out," Audrey said. "We have one chance in five, since there are twenty-five kids in our class."

Marvin slurped some milk, then
joined the conversation. "Three of the
lucky winners should be boys, since we

have sixteen boys and nine girls in our room."

Mary crunched on a carrot. "Who knows? Muh-maybe it will be four girls and one boy."

Marvin shook his head. "Impossible."

Just before they went outside to play, Mary remembered something.

"Ooops! I forgot muh-my jacket, Audrey. I'll run upstairs and get it. See you outside."

"See you! I'll save you a place in the tetherball line."

"Thanks," Mary said, and then she got permission from the lunch aide to go back to her classroom.

As she walked up the stairs and down the hall, Mary noticed how quiet everything in the building was at noontime. The secretary was on the phone, but no

one else was in the office. All the teachers were at the end of the hall, eating lunch in the teachers' room.

When Mary got to the coatrack, no one was around. She pulled her jacket off the hanger and then peeked into her classroom. All the candy bars were still on the desks.

Mary started thinking about her candy bar. *Ohhh!* she thought. If she had that golden ticket, she could have lunch with her favorite teacher. What harm would it be to peek at her own? Mary couldn't stand it any longer.

She stepped into the room and hurried over to her desk. With one quick motion, she slid the silver foil out of its brown wrapper.

Mary closed her eyes and then unfolded the two sides of foil.

Be there! she thought.

Slowly, she opened her eyes.

Dark chocolate.

Nothing else.

Mary's heart sank. No golden ticket! What a disappointment.

When Mary turned, she noticed Marvin's desk. If he didn't get a golden ticket, Mary knew she would feel better.

One quick peek?

It was so tempting!

Yes!

Quickly, she stepped over to Marvin's desk and picked up his candy bar. Once again she slid the foil from inside the brown wrapper. As she unfolded the shiny paper, she saw something sparkle in the November sunlight that filtered through the window.

A golden ticket!

Marvin had one in his candy bar!

How could he be so lucky a third time?

Mary stomped her foot. It wasn't fair! Marvin would brag to everyone about getting the golden ticket. Then he would burp and make a mess of the pizza and sundae treats. He might even sing one of his mean songs about Mrs. Bird. Marvin would spoil the fun for everyone. Especially for their teacher!

Mary looked at Marvin's candy bar.

Ohhhhh, she thought. *It would be so easy to . . .*

No, Mary didn't want to think it.

She wrapped the bar back up.

It wasn't right.

Mary turned and trudged toward the door. Why did Marvin have to get the golden ticket?

Then Mary stopped.

Who knew Marvin had it?

Just her.

She could make things better.

She could make things fair.

She could make Mrs. Bird happy.

Mary looked up at the clock. Only a few minutes had passed. No one would suspect a thing.

Slowly, Mary turned around and walked back to her desk.

She looked at her candy bar.

She looked at Marvin's.

Then Mary *did it*.
She switched candy bars with Marvin.
And raced outside to the playground.

4

Golden Discoveries!

When the noon recess bell rang, Mrs. Bird's class was the first to line up. They couldn't wait to get back to their classroom.

"I'm putting chocolate sauce on my sundae," Marvin joked. "And lots of sprinkles!"

Mary glared at him. How could he be so sure he had a golden ticket?

Audrey kept jumping. "I hope one of us gets to go!" she said.

Mary didn't feel like jumping. Her stomach was starting to feel funny. "I think I ate too muh-muh-many chicken nuggets."

Audrey put her arm around her friend. "I don't think so! We hardly touched our food. We were too ex-cited!"

"I . . . I just don't feel well."

Mary dragged her feet as the rest of her class hurried down the hall.

"You and me!" Marvin said to Fred. "I feel it in my bones. We're going to be lucky today."

"I *hope* I am!" Fred said.

Mary sank down in her seat. She couldn't bring herself to open her candy bar. She already knew what was inside.

Maybe it was the fresh air at recess. Maybe it was her conscience. Mary knew what she didn't know thirty minutes ago.

What she did was wrong.

Very wrong.

Marvin leaned back in his seat. "I'll wait awhile too, Muh-muh-mary," he said.

Mary felt a tear roll down one side of her cheek. It was a warm one, and when she caught it with her tongue, it tasted like salt.

Mrs. Bird stopped at Mary's desk. "Are you okay?"

Mary nodded.

But she wasn't. She felt horrible.

"Thank you for your thoughtful note, Mary," Mrs. Bird said. "It made my day!"

Mary tried to smile, but it was hard. She knew she wasn't going to make her teacher's day *today*.

Mary had cheated.

For the very first time.

And it felt awful.

"Here's Elizabeth's bar," Mrs. Bird said. "You can take it to her."

Mary looked at the second candy bar on her desk. Suddenly, she got a powerful idea. She could give her candy bar to Elizabeth! Then Elizabeth would have the golden ticket.

Mary started unwrapping the bar

Mrs. Bird had just put on her desk.

Marvin started unwrapping his, too. "Now, Muh-muh-mary, I don't want you to be too disappointed when I pull out my golden ticket."

Mary looked over at Marvin. "You think you know everything!" she blurted out.

Marvin grinned. "Just watch!"

Mary did.

After he unfolded the silver foil, his wide smile dropped. "HUH? How could that be?"

Mary looked back at her own bar. She wished she could enjoy Marvin's disappointment more. But she didn't. She still felt guilty.

Mary slid the foil out and then opened it. A tint of gold sparkled before her. Elizabeth's had a golden ticket, too!

Marvin leaned over the aisle. "YOU CHEATED, MARY MARONY!"

Now Mary's stomach hurt even more.

"You took my golden ticket!"

Mary looked straight ahead. She was in a daze.

"I GOT ONE!" Pablo yelled. Then he stood up and read what it said:

GOLDEN GREETINGS

THIS TICKET IS

GOOD FOR ONE LUNCH

WITH THE TEACHER

NOV. 10TH.

"Me too!" Amol replied, jumping up and down.

"I have one!" Emmy Sue said.

"That's three. . . ." Mrs. Bird counted. "Where are the other two?"

Audrey leaped out of her seat. "MARY HAS A GOLDEN TICKET!"

Marvin folded his arms and sank down in his seat. "I was robbed!"

"Well, congratulations!" Mrs. Bird said. "That means Elizabeth Conway has the fifth golden ticket. What a surprise. And it was the candy bar no one wanted."

As the teacher wrote the five winners on the board, half the class cheered.

Half sighed.

Marvin kept mumbling, "Mary cheated."

When Mrs. Bird turned around, she noticed Mary had her head down. She walked over to Mary's desk and gently tapped her shoulder. "I'm so happy you got a golden ticket!" she whispered.

Mary wanted to look up at her teacher and blurt out the truth, but if she did, Mrs. Bird would know she had cheated. Her favorite teacher would be so disappointed in her.

It wouldn't be Marvin this time that gave Mrs. Bird more gray hair, Mary thought. *It would be me.*

5

Stomachaches

When Mary got to Elizabeth's house, she took a deep breath, counted to ten, and tried to think just about her friend, not the golden ticket.

Mrs. Conway answered the door. "Hello, Mary."

"Hello, Muh-mrs. Conway. How's Elizabeth?"

"Well, she says she has a bad stomach-ache, but I have a feeling something else is bothering her. She's been on the couch all day. She hasn't eaten much. Want to visit awhile?"

"Y-yes."

Mrs. Conway took Mary into their living room, where Elizabeth was lying on the couch with a blanket and pillow

and their dog, Tucker. Half a bowl of chicken soup was on the coffee table.

"I'll get you girls some crackers and ginger ale," Mrs. Conway said.

As soon as she left the room, Mary sat on the floor next to Elizabeth.

"What's wrong, Lizzy?"

"Oh, Mary," Elizabeth groaned. "I . . . I've got this gross disease."

"What is it?"

"I don't know. That's the spooky part. It just looks gross."

"Where is it?" Mary asked.

"Plug your nose first," Elizabeth said.

Mary plugged her nose.

Elizabeth sat up and took her purple fluffy slipper off. Then she pulled her toes apart. "See? It's all yucky and crusty in there."

"Eweyee," Mary said.

"And it's itchy," Elizabeth added.

"Did you show your muh-mom?"
Mary asked.

"No!"

"Why not?"

"Because she'll put on that orange
stuff that stings."

"You muh-mean Muh-merthiolate?"

"That's it."

Mary looked again. "I've seen that disease before."

"You have?"

"Muh-muh-my dad gets it."

"What's it called?"

"Athlete's foot. People who play sports get it."

Elizabeth thought about it. "Well, I am an athlete. I play kickball and tetherball."

"You're a great athlete," Mary added. "Great athletes get toes like yours."

"Does your dad put that orange stuff on?" Elizabeth still couldn't remember the word for it.

"No. He has a special powder. It even smells good."

Mrs. Conway came into the living room. "You're looking better, Elizabeth. Maybe you just needed a visit from a friend."

When the phone rang, Mrs. Conway set her tray on the coffee table and returned to the kitchen. Elizabeth reached for a glass of ginger ale and some crackers.

"Are you going to tell your muh-mom about your toes now?" Mary asked.

Elizabeth nodded. "Yes. I don't like it when I have to tell a lie."

Mary nodded back. She knew about lies. There were the small white ones that were okay once in a while. Sometimes you said them to be polite. Like if you hated someone's birthday cupcake at school but pretended to love it. And then there were the real ones.

Elizabeth crunched on a cracker. "So, what happened in school today?" she asked.

Mary immediately thought about her cheating. Was that a lie? If it was, she wondered what color it would be.

When Mary didn't say anything, Elizabeth asked another question.

"Do we have any homework?"

Mary didn't mind telling Elizabeth about the homework. "You h-have to wr-write six 'I notice' s-sentences. It can b-be about anything."

"You mean like . . . 'I noticed Tucker took a lick of my chicken soup'?"

"Yeah." Mary smiled.

Slowly, Mary pulled the candy bar out of her bookbag. She couldn't avoid the subject any longer. Mary explained the special activity that celebrated *Charlie and the Chocolate Factory*. "If you h-have a g-golden ticket inside, you're one of the f-five lucky w-winners."

Mary put her head down. Her speech therapist told her she'd stutter more when she was upset.

"What fun!" Elizabeth said, sliding the brown wrapper off. "I remember who got the golden tickets in the book—Charlie Bucket, Mike Teavee, Augustus Gloop, Violet Beauregarde, Veruca Salt . . . and . . . ME!

"I GOT A GOLDEN TICKET!"

Elizabeth got up and started jumping on the couch. "I GET TO HAVE PIZZA WITH MRS. BIRD! YIPPEE!" Then she added, "Who else won?"

"Muh-me . . ." Mary replied softly.

"YOU?" Elizabeth waved her golden ticket in the air. "DOUBLE YIPPEE!!!! YOU GOT LUCKY, TOO!"

"Y-yes," Mary said.

When her ache came back, Mary knew why.

She had just told a big fat fib to her best friend. Cheating *was* lying! It wasn't a white one either. It was black and blue like a bruise. And sore.

Elizabeth stopped jumping and stared at Mary. "How come you're not excited?"

Mary didn't say anything. She looked over at Tucker, who was wagging his tail and sniffing the tray.

Elizabeth plopped down on the couch. "Huh?" she said. "You haven't even touched your ginger ale or crackers either."

Mary turned and looked at her friend. She wanted to tell her the truth so badly. Elizabeth always understood. They shared everything. Secrets about

49

hating Marvin and toe diseases. But if Mary told her about cheating, it would just spoil things for Elizabeth.

"Are you okay?"

Mary shook her head. "I . . . think I have a stomachache."

Just then Mrs. Conway returned to the living room. "That was your mother, Mary. She wanted to know where you were. She wants you to come home. She has something to tell you."

"I b-better go," Mary said.

Then she picked up her bookbag and ran out of the house.

6

Time-out at Home

As Mary ran home, she thought about what she could do.

Tell her mother.

Her mother could call Mrs. Bird and explain everything for her. Mrs. Bird would forgive her and everything would be okay.

Yes!

Mary leaped over the cracks on the

sidewalk, then skipped steps up to her house.

When she got inside, she dropped her bookbag.

What was going on?

A huge sign that went from one end of the living room to the other had large red Magic Marker letters that said:

I'M A CHEF!

"MARY!" Mrs. Marony called as she rushed to the door. "Finally, you're home. *This* is a special day. I got a job!"

Mary went over to the hall closet and hung up her jacket. This was not the time for her black-and-blue lie. It was the time for little white ones.

"I'm happy for you, Mom!"

When Mrs. Marony hugged Mary, it was so tight it almost made the ache go away.

"Where's your job, Mom?"

"The Hacienda! That new restaurant on the green. They need extra help for the holidays."

"What do you cook?" Mary asked. She kept hugging her mother back.

"You'll find out tonight," Mrs. Marony said. "I'm making one of their specialties. Want to help me decorate

the kitchen so we can surprise your
father?"

"Sure."

At five-thirty on the nose, when Mr.
Marony came in the front door, the
house was dark.

"Anyone home?" he called.

Mary and her mother hid under the
kitchen table.

"HELLOOOOOOOO?"

When Mr. Marony flicked on the
lights, he saw the big sign.

"YOU GOT A JOB!" he yelled. "Now,
where's that chef and her assistant?"

Mr. Marony looked in the bedrooms.

Mary giggled under the table. She
loved it when her father played games.

"NOT HERE!" he yelled. "I THINK
I'LL LOOK IN THE BATHROOM."

Now both Mary and Mrs. Marony
giggled.

"COULD THEY POSSIBLY BE . . .
IN THE . . . *KITCHEN?*"

As soon as he flicked on the kitchen
lights, Mary and her mother yelled,
"SURPRISE!" And they popped out
from the table.

"All *right!*" Mr. Marony said, hugging them both. "This is a celebration!"

After Mary's parents chatted about the job, they all sat down at the table.

The enchilada dish sat on a wooden chopping board in the middle of the table.

"Mmmmm, I can smell the tomatoes, onion, and green peppers," Mr. Marony said, scooping some on their plates.

Mary looked at the melted cheese that dripped from his spoon.

Mrs. Marony passed a bowl of guacamole. "Don't forget this!"

The only conversation that night at the table was "Mmmmm . . ."

"Mmmmmm . . ."

And "Mmmmmmm."

That suited Mary just fine.

However, later that night, when her

mother tucked her in bed, Mary was reminded of school.

"Did you get your homework done?"

"Yes. Dad helped muh-me spell some of the words."

"Good. Try to get some sleep now."

Mary liked it when her mother kissed her three times on her forehead. It gave her courage.

Mary needed it.

Tomorrow *she* would have to tell the teacher and the class about the terrible thing she did.

And that's what worried Mary. The telling part. What if she had a stuttering attack and couldn't get the words out? Miss Lawton, her speech therapist at school, told her she was making wonderful progress, and she needed to see her only once a week.

But Mary knew sometimes it was harder for her to talk.

This was one of those times.

7

Mary Tells the Truth

Mary sat in her seat the next morning, shivering.

She avoided Audrey and Elizabeth. Right now they were busy feeding Fluffy some lettuce.

Mary pretended to write in her notebook. No one knew she was just scribbling O's.

"Mornin', cheater," Marvin snapped

when he sat down in the desk behind her.

Mary quickly turned the page. Marvin would notice the O's. He peeked at everything.

"I hope you're enjoying my golden ticket," he sneered.

Mary looked at Marvin and then at the agenda on the board. Mrs. Bird wanted the children to read their "I notice" homework sentences aloud.

Mary suddenly smiled.

Yes! she thought.

"You know what?" Marvin bugged. "You're nothing but a big fat cheater."

Mary ignored Marvin and everyone else. She had something more important to do.

After the bell, pledge, song, and lunch count, Mrs. Bird said, "Take out your homework, please. I want you to read your six sentences in the Teacher's Chair."

Mrs. Bird got her grade book and sat in the back of the room. "Last time we started with A, so today we'll start with Z. Pablo Zapato, you're first."

Emmy Sue Aiken frowned. She was last.

Mary smiled. She still had time to finish. She was glad *Marony* was in the middle of the alphabet.

Five minutes later, Audrey Tang took her turn in the Teacher's Chair.

"I noticed Fluffy's long hair covers his eyes."

The class turned and looked back at the guinea pig.

"I noticed Mary wasn't very happy when she got her golden ticket."

Everyone looked at Mary.

She was busy writing.

"I noticed . . ." Audrey continued, "Marvin peeked at his chocolate bar yesterday."

Now everyone looked at Marvin.

"I DIDN'T PEEK!" he shouted.

"Shhhhhh!" Mrs. Bird replied. "It's Audrey's turn to talk."

"I noticed Marvin was sour grapes when he found out he wasn't a winner."

Mrs. Bird raised her eyebrows.

Audrey read her last sentence. "I notice there's a cobweb on the ceiling."
Everyone looked up.

"Over there." Marvin pointed. "Above Mrs. Bird's desk!"

"Oh my goodness!" Mrs. Bird said. "Just look at that beautiful miracle of nature."

"Ooooooooooh," everyone oohed.

Except Mary.

She was still writing.

Five minutes later, Mrs. Bird said, "Mary Marony, it's your turn."

Mary didn't take the homework paper she had worked on with her dad. She took her notebook. Slowly, she walked to the front of the room and sat down in the big Teacher's Chair.

Her feet dangled just above the floor. Her elbows rested on the big wooden arms of the chair.

Mary was so glad she didn't stutter when she whispered, sang, or *read* things.

"Yesterday . . ."

"Would you read a little louder?" Mrs. Bird said. "Thank you, Mary."

Mary cleared her throat.

"Yesterday at lunch recess, I came back to the room for my jacket. I noticed the candy bars on all the desks."

The class was pin-drop quiet.

Marvin leaned forward.

"I especially noticed my candy bar. I went over and . . . peeked."

Mrs. Bird put her pen down and listened with her eyes as well as her ears.

"I noticed my . . . chocolate bar didn't have a golden ticket."

The class gasped.

Audrey fiddled with her necklace.

Elizabeth raised her eyebrows.

Mary kept looking at her notebook. "I noticed Marvin's candy bar. I thought I would feel better if he didn't have a golden ticket. So I peeked in Marvin's.''

Mary looked up at the teacher's sad face.

Then she continued. "I didn't want Marvin to win because he might spoil things. So . . . I switched candy bars. The golden ticket I have . . . is . . . Marvin's.''

"I KNEW IT!" Marvin blurted out. "SHE CHEATED!"

Mrs. Bird didn't say anything. She just set her grade book aside and walked toward the front of the room.

Mary put her head down and started crying. "I'm . . . ruh-real . . . sor-sor-sorry.''

Mrs. Bird put her arm around Mary. "I'm glad you told us the truth.''

Marvin sang out, "She's going to get in BIG, BIG trouble!''

Mrs. Bird looked at the class. "Mary told us the truth. That's punishment enough. It takes courage to admit you did something wrong and to say you're sorry."

Marvin shrugged. "Man, she got off easy. Hey, where's my golden ticket?"

Mary walked over to Marvin's desk and handed it to him. "I'm sorry . . . Muh-muh-marvin."

Marvin looked at the golden ticket on his desk. "That's . . . okay . . . Mare."

Mary was surprised Marvin didn't call her "Muh-muh-mary."

After she wiped her eyes, Mary looked over at her two best friends. *Do they hate me?* she wondered.

Audrey shook her head as she talked with Pablo. "I would never cheat. It's not right. I hope Mary learned her lesson."

Elizabeth looked at the E word on their chart. *Empathy.* She had empathy for Mary. She knew how Mary felt. Elizabeth got out of her chair and went over and hugged Mary. "I'm glad we both finally told the truth."

Mrs. Bird sat down on a desk. "We're like a family, class. We share the good things and the bad. No one's perfect."

Mary exchanged smiles with Mrs. Bird and Elizabeth. They understood.

"Can we get back to our sentences now?" Fred Heinz asked.

Mrs. Bird got up and walked to the back of the room. "Yes, let's. Marvin Higgins, you're next."

"I . . . I left my homework at home."

Mrs. Bird frowned and recorded a zero.

"I'm next," Fred said, racing for the Teacher's Chair. "The truth about Marvin's golden ticket is not all out. Not the WHOLE TRUTH."

"There's more?" Mrs. Bird replied.

Fred looked over at Marvin. "Yes . . . *lots* more!"

"*Fred!*" Marvin groaned. "You better not . . ."

8

The Fifth Golden-Ticket Holder

Fred didn't have to wait for rude people, like he usually did when it was his turn to share his homework.

Everyone was quiet.

"Mary got me thinking," Fred began. "Now I want to tell the truth, too."

Marvin raised one finger.

That meant he was asking for permission to go to the bathroom.

Mrs. Bird shook her head. "We *all* need to hear what Fred has to say."

Marvin made a face.

Fred took out a piece of wrinkled paper. "I wrote these sentences after Mary read her homework."

Mrs. Bird nodded her approval.

"Yesterday I noticed Marvin peeked at his Hershey bar."

Marvin started to squirm in his seat.

"I noticed he ripped the foil in one corner. When we were lining up for lunch, Marvin wasn't in the hall. So I went back in the room to get him. Marvin said he was getting his milk money. But I noticed his candy bar didn't have a little tear in the corner anymore. Mary's did."

Everyone groaned and looked at Marvin.

He was sinking down in his seat.

Mrs. Bird stood up and waited.

The room was pin-drop quiet.

"OKAY!" Marvin yelled. "I SWITCHED CANDY BARS WITH MARY. She did the same thing to me."

Mary turned around and looked at Marvin. "You muh-mean, I had a golden ticket all along?"

"Yeah. I . . . switched candy bars with you before lunchtime."

"And . . ." Mrs. Bird was still waiting.

Marvin shrugged. "What? I told the truth."

"Are you sorry?" Mrs. Bird asked.

Marvin mumbled something.

"I didn't hear you, Marvin. Don't you think you owe Mary and the class an apology?"

"I'm sorry," Marvin snapped.

"You're not showing much remorse," Mrs. Bird said. "You sound like you don't mean it."

"So? I'm not a crybaby like Mary."

"I'm not asking for tears, Marvin. Just sincerity."

Mrs. Bird went over to the big chart and added two new words:

Remorse.

Sincere.

Fred pointed to the S word. "Is that

like 'Sincerely yours' in letters?"

"Yes," Mrs. Bird replied. "Now, class, how many of you thought Mary was sincere when she apologized about switching the tickets?"

Everyone raised a hand except Marvin.

Suddenly Marvin jumped up.

"What about me? How many of you thought I was sincere?"

Marvin turned around to see who raised a hand.

Nobody.

Not even his best friend, Fred.

Marvin plopped down in his chair. "No one likes me."

Mrs. Bird came over and patted Marvin's shoulder. "That's not true. We *do* like you, Marvin. We're just disappointed you don't *sound* like you're

sorry. You sound like you don't care."

Marvin looked up at his classmates. He could tell they were waiting.

Slowly, he reached in his desk and got a piece of scratch paper.

And started writing.

When he was finished he handed it to Mrs. Bird.

The teacher smiled when she read it. "Mary, would you read this aloud, please? It's to you."

Mary took the paper and started reading. It said:

Dear Mary,
I'm sorry I took your tikit.
It was a ratin thing to do.
I hope you injoy that piza.
Pleas save me a slis or two.

Sincere Marvin

When everyone started clapping and laughing, Marvin smiled. The class liked his poem of apology.

Mary leaned back and smiled too, but for her own reasons.

Mary's conscience was clear and her ache was gone. That was better than anything gold she held in her hand.

EPILOGUE
Pizza and Poems

"Where is that pizza?" Mrs. Bird asked.

Mary and the other four children looked up at the classroom clock. They had only twenty minutes left to eat.

"Maybe we should have the dessert first," Pablo suggested.

"Yeah!" Amol agreed.

The teacher shook her head. "I guess we'll have to."

Everyone watched Mrs. Bird open the red cooler. There was a giant carton of ice cream on top of the ice block, jars of marshmallow cream, chocolate fudge sauce, and caramel sauce, strawberries, a giant can of whipped cream, and a little jar of maraschino cherries.

"Help yourself," Mrs. Bird said, scooping the ice cream into paper bowls. "So . . ." she said, "what was your favorite invention at Wonka's factory?"

Emmy Sue answered first, after she wiped some marshmallow cream off her mouth. "Exploding candy for your enemies."

Mary licked chocolate off her lips. "Fizzy Lifting Lemonade Swimming Pools."

Pablo waved his spoon in the air.

"Luminous Lollipops for eating in bed at night."

Amol shouted, "INVISIBLE CHOCOLATE BARS FOR EATING IN CLASS."

Mrs. Bird laughed. Then she heard someone at the door. "Is that the pizza?"

"I'm afraid not," said Mr. Woods, the school librarian. "I just stopped by to see how the golden-ticket holders were doing."

"GREAT!" the children replied.

"Not really," Mrs. Bird said. "The pizza hasn't arrived yet and my class will be returning soon."

Mr. Woods smiled. "Well, I guess you'll have to move your party to the library."

"The library?" Pablo repeated.

"Sure."

"You don't mind?" Mrs. Bird asked.

"Not at all. Besides, my next class doesn't come until after one."

"You're a lifesaver!" Mrs. Bird said.

Mr. Woods rubbed his hands together. "I'm also hungry."

Just then a delivery boy wearing a red cap appeared at the door. "Is this Mrs. Bird's room?"

"YES!"

"Sorry I'm late. I went to the wrong school. Where do you want the two double-cheese pizzas?"

"I'll take them," Mr. Woods said. Then he pointed to Mrs. Bird. "She's paying."

Minutes later, everyone was sitting at a library table eating pizza, drinking fizzy-lifting lemonade, and talking about the book *Charlie and the Chocolate Factory*.

"So what's your favorite invention from Wonka's factory, Muh-mr. Woods?" Mary asked.

The librarian put down his slice of pizza. "That's easy. Rainbow Drops. Suck them and you can spit in different colors."

Everyone laughed so hard they didn't even notice the bell.

Mary took a big gulp of fizzy-lifting lemonade.

And then she did it.

"*BUUUUUUUURRRRP!*"

All eyes stared at Mary.

"*Excuse muh-me*," she said, covering her mouth. "I can't believe I did that!"

"I CAN! WAY TO GO, MARE!" said a voice from the hall.

Mary turned. Her class was passing by. Marvin was in the doorway with his thumbs up.

Mary covered her face with her empty paper plate.

"This really is a celebration," Marvin said. "It calls for a poem. Ready?"

"Ready!" Pablo called back.

Marvin closed his eyes and waited for inspiration. "Got it!"

I used to think my favorite
Was good ol' Wyatt Earp.
But now it's Mary Marony
'Cause she did the biggest burp!

Pablo and Amol clapped.

Marvin took a bow and asked, "So where's my slice of pizza?"

Mary set her plate down.

And slowly got up.

"I do poetry, too," she said. "Ready?"

"Ready." Marvin beamed.

Thanks to your poem, Marvin,
You're going back to class starvin'.

Then Mary closed the door.
And smiled.